The Hermit

Tarot Card Notebook

Shop More Designs Like This at
www.theghoulishgarb.com

All rights reserved. No part of this book may be reproduced, stored in a retrieval system, or transmitted in any form or by any means, electronic, mechanical, photocopying, recording, or otherwise, without the prior written permission of the author, except as provided by U.S.A. copyright law.

The Hermit: Tarot Card Notebook
© 2019 The Ghoulish Garb

This Book Belongs To

THE HERMIT.

Made in United States
Orlando, FL
17 October 2024